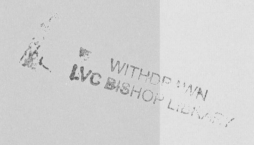

For ladies and
gentlemen
and children
of all ages

One
seed
in the
ground,
three
miles
out of
town.

One fast-growing tree where the seed used to be.

3 CHIPMUNKS

2 SPARROWS

A WHOPPING BIG BEE

all live in the tree where the seed used to be.

A chicken.

Two blue jays, three squirrels, a clown,

A CAT WHO CLIMBED UP BUT CAN'T FIND HER WAY DOWN,

3 CHIPMUNKS,

TWO SPARROWS,

A WHOPPING BIG BEE,

five mice AND A Raven

all live in the tree.

The traveling circus of

looks up and looks down for their runaway clown.

Because they both stare at the tree, they don't see
that two clever apes are stealing their key.

One
rolling
circus
rolls
off
once
again.

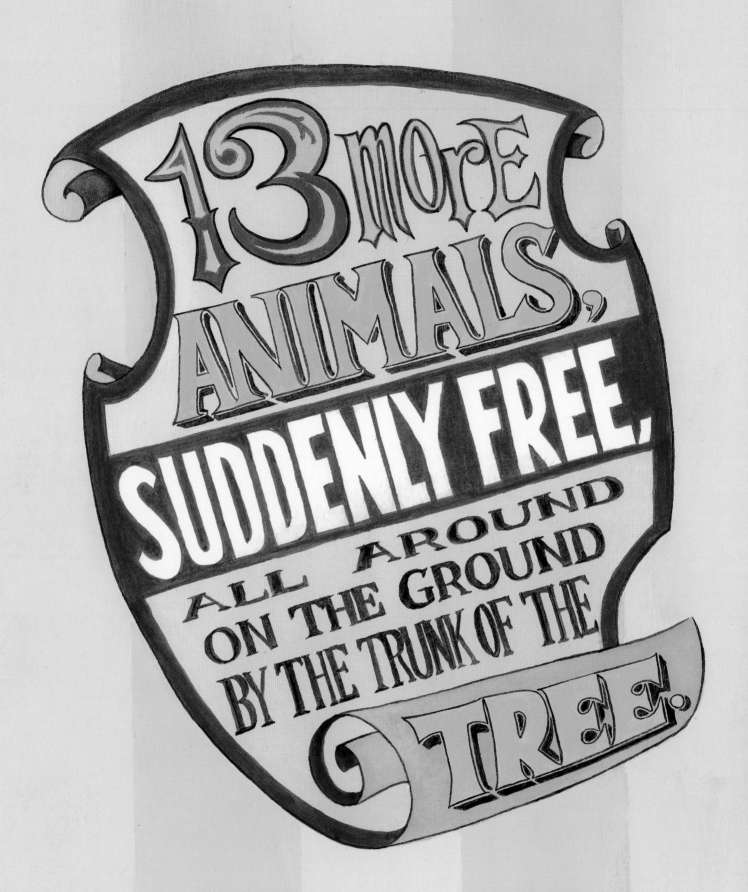

2 tigers

three chip-munks

FIVE
POODLES WITH CAPES

ONE LION

3 squirrels

2 key-stealing APES

two blue jays

ONE OSTRICH

ONE RAVEN

...and a very full tree.

And one elephant.

Drumroll, please.

Whoops.

Thirty-three animals,
counting the clown,
get up off the ground
without making a sound,

and flee from the lea
where a tree used to be,

until it fell down,

three miles out of town.

Thanks to Tamson and Marie
for their thoughtfulness and help
—A.R.

www.HarcourtBooks.com

Library of Congress Cataloging-in-Publication Data
Rex, Adam.
Tree-ring circus/Adam Rex.
p. cm.
Summary: In this cumulative tale, a tree becomes a hiding place
for various animals, a runaway circus clown, and even an elephant.
[1. Trees—Fiction. 2. Animals—Fiction. 3. Clowns—Fiction.
4. Circus—Fiction. 5. Counting. 6. Stories in rhyme.] I. Title.
PZ8.3.R3177Tr 2006
[E]—dc22   2004015849
ISBN-13: 978-0152-05363-5 ISBN-10: 0-15-205363-8

First edition
A C E G H F D B

The illustrations in this book were done in oils and mixed media on paper.
The display type was created by Judythe Sieck.
The text type was set in Clarendon.
Color separations by Bright Arts Ltd., Hong Kong
Manufactured by SNP Leefung Holdings Limited, China
This book was printed on totally chlorine-free Stora Enso Matte paper.
Production supervision by Ginger Boyer
Designed by Adam Rex, Kristine Brogno, and Scott Piehl

No animals were harmed in the making of this book.
The cat complained of neck pain, but was later found to be faking.